29848
Fateful Forebodings (Secrets of the Unexplained)
Gary L. Blackwood
AR B.L.: 7.2
Points: 1.0   UG

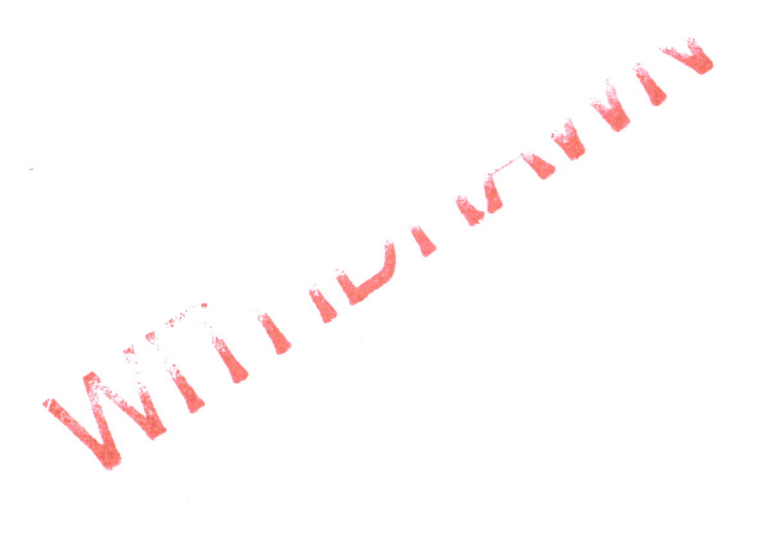

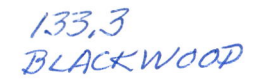

SECRETS OF THE UNEXPLAINED

Fateful Forebodings

by Gary L. Blackwood

BENCHMARK BOOKS

MARSHALL CAVENDISH
NEW YORK

Benchmark Books
Marshall Cavendish Corporation
99 White Plains Road
Tarrytown, New York 10591

Copyright © 1999 by Marshall Cavendish Corporation
All rights reserved. No part of this book may be reproduced in any form
without written permission from the publisher.

Library of Congress Cataloging-in-Publication Data
Blackwood, Gary L.
Fateful forebodings / by Gary L. Blackwood.
p. cm. — (Secrets of the unexplained)
Includes bibliographical references and index.
Summary: Describes some of the ways humans have tried to foretell the future
throughout history and discusses specific instances of such prophecies.
ISBN 0-7614-0467-8
1. Prophecies (Occultism)—Juvenile literature. 2. Precognition—Juvenile literature.
[1. Prophecies (Occultism) 2. Precognition.]
I. Title. II. Series: Blackwood, Gary L. Secrets of the unexplained.
BF1791.B53   1999   133.3—dc21   97-11078 CIP   AC

Photo Credits: Front cover: courtesy of Peter Holst/The Image Bank, Inc.; back cover: courtesy of The British Museum/Rainbird/Robert Harding; page 6: Archive Photos; pages 8-9, 13, 17, 18, 31, 35, 41: ©Charles Walker Collection/Stock Montage, Inc.; page 14: ©Derrick Witty/George Rainbird Ltd., British Museum; page 15: Joyce Stanton; page 16: Bridgeman/Art Resource, NY; page 21: Stock Montage, Inc.; page 24-25: Scala/Art Resource, NY; page 27 (top): The London Times/Archive Photos; (bottom): By permission of the British Library (Ms. Add. Meladius, 12228, fol. 202v); page 28: Mary Evans Picture Library/Photo by Courau; page 36: Corbis-Bettman; pages 37, 51, 57, 66: UPI/Corbis-Bettman; page 44: Philip Panton/Fortean Picture Library; pages 46-47, 60: Mary Evans Picture Library; page 52-53: Mitch Blank/Archive Photos; page 71: Alfred Gescheidt/The Image Bank; page 72: Elle Schuster/The Image Bank

Printed in Hong Kong

3 5 6 4 2

Contents

Introduction   5

PART ONE
Prophecy

Tricks of the Trade   11

Greeks Bearing Gifts   20

Emperors and Kings   23

Ten Centuries' Worth of Prophecy   30

Poor Prophets   34

How to Be a Prophet   39

PART TWO
Premonitions

Violent Visions   49

Ignoring the Message   55

Listening to the Message   59

Seeing Around the Bend   65

Changing the Future   70

Glossary   73

To Learn More about Telling the Future   76

Index   78

Introduction

Wouldn't it be great if you could look into the future? You could make a million dollars by foreseeing the winning lottery numbers. You'd know in advance what college you're going to and what career you'll pursue; that means you wouldn't have to waste time studying all those subjects you won't need. You'd see whether or not you'll get married, and to whom. You'd know how books and movies are going to end, and whether your team will win the Super Bowl or the World Series, and what you're going to get for your birthday and Christmas. . . .

Well, maybe it wouldn't be so great after all. A lot of the fun in life comes from *not* knowing what's going to happen.

It doesn't matter, anyway, because no one can really see into the future, right? All we can know is what's already happened. No one can possibly see something that hasn't happened yet, right?

Don't be so sure.

Ever since humans have been aware that there is a future, we've been trying to catch a glimpse of it. And occasionally people seem to actually do so. Sometimes they're deliberately trying to read the future. That's called prophecy or prediction. Sometimes it happens by

If you anticipate an unpleasant fate, shouldn't you be able to take steps to avoid it? The Greek poet Aeschylus thought so. He was dead wrong.

INTRODUCTION

accident. That's called precognition or premonition.

(Technically, there is a distinction between these last two terms. *Precognition* means seeing an event unfold in full, realistic detail; a *premonition* is more of a vague feeling that something is going to happen. But for convenience in this book, we'll lump both terms under the heading of *premonition*. Sometimes there's also a distinction made between *prophecy*, used to refer mainly to large-scale events, and *prediction*, which may cover only one person's future. But again for convenience, we'll put them both under the heading of *prophecy*.)

Some people who receive these visions of the future choose to ignore them. Others take advantage of the early warning and avoid or alter their fate. Still others try to change the way the future looks, and fail miserably.

In the fifth century B.C. the Greek poet Aeschylus determined that, according to the stars, on a certain day he'd die as the result of a heavy object dropping on his head. In an attempt to cheat fate, Aeschylus fled to a barren desert where, he thought, nothing could possibly fall on him. But as he sat on the sand, surrounded by emptiness, a bird flew over, carrying a turtle. Mistaking Aeschylus's bald head for a rock, it dropped the turtle on him, cracking his skull.

A twelfth-century astrologer named Michael Scot foresaw a similar fate for himself, and carefully avoided any place where an object was likely to brain him. While he was praying in a cathedral, a stone dislodged from the ceiling and hit him dead center.

Scot's fellow astrologer Franciscus Junctinus, expecting a violent death at a certain day and hour, locked himself in his library—and was crushed beneath an avalanche of his own books.

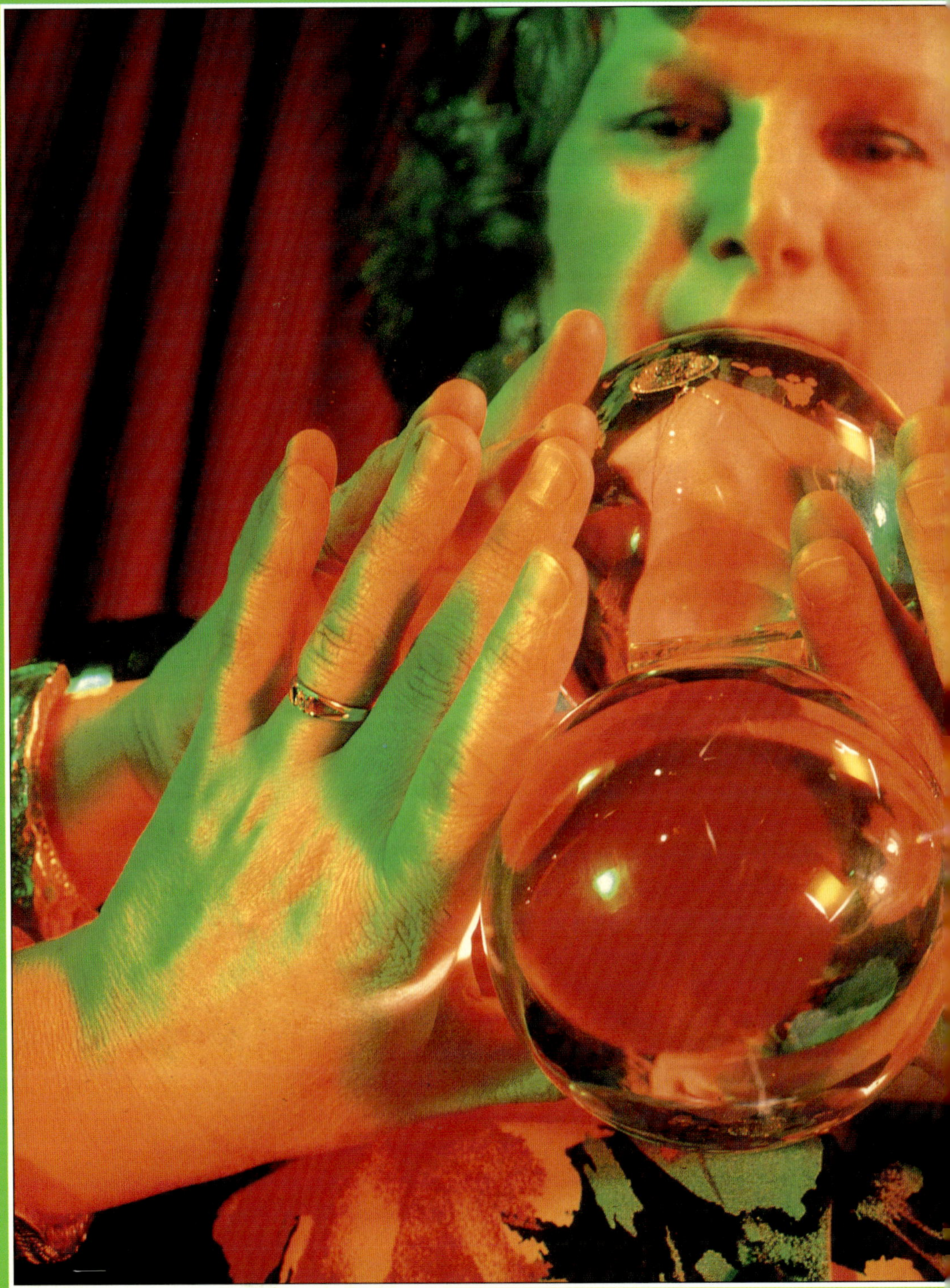

PART ONE

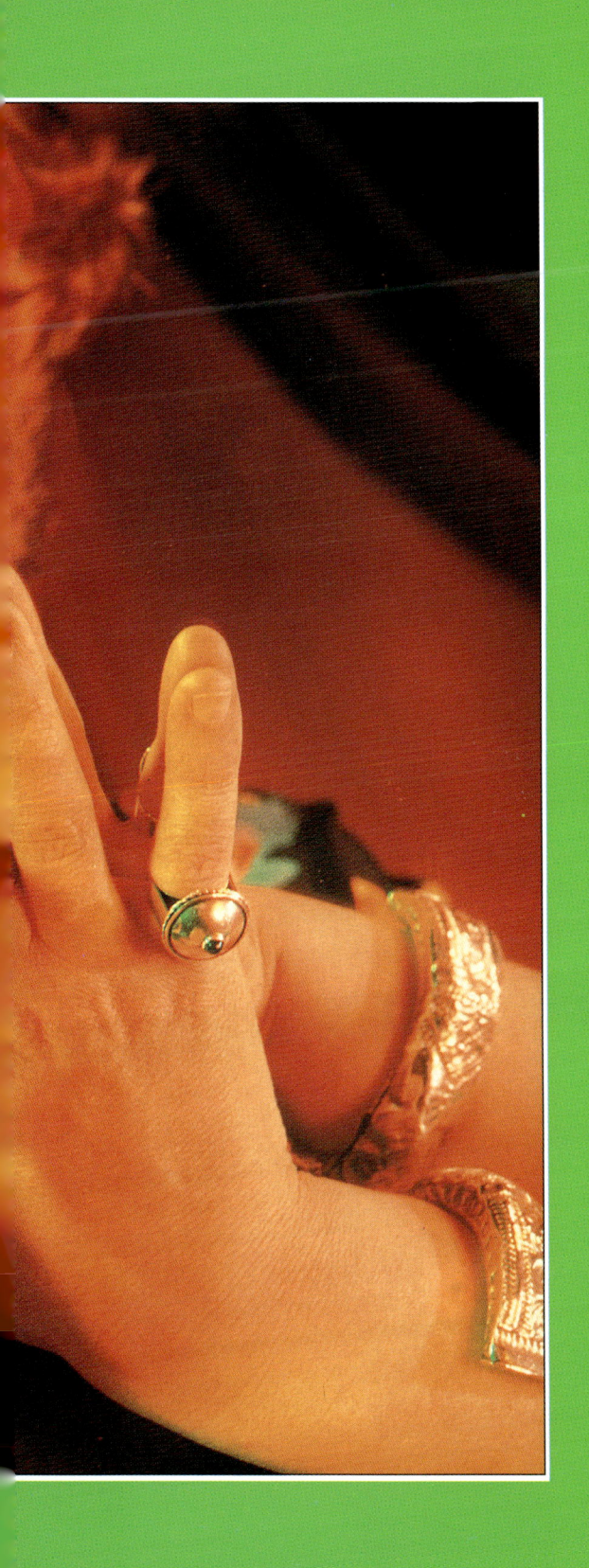

Prophecy

Tricks of the Trade

There's evidence that all of us have the ability to send out feelers into the future. But just as some of us have a natural aptitude for music or math or mechanics, some are better than others at tuning in to those mysterious messages about things to come. Those rare individuals have been around as long as humankind has, and we've given them a variety of names: psychics, prophets, seers, soothsayers, oracles.

When they get their information wrong, or are just faking it, we give them less flattering names, such as frauds and charlatans.

Naturally, there have been far more poor and phony prophets than there have been genuine and accurate ones. Both the fakes and the true prophets have used a mind-boggling array of devices to help them tell the future: animal guts and bones, moldy cheese, fig leaves, the shapes of clouds, snakes, urine, a boiled donkey's head, hysterical laughter, the behavior of cats, rose petals, even the air or the earth itself.

Fads in fortune-telling have come and gone, but several tried-and-true methods have been in constant use for centuries.

FATEFUL FOREBODINGS

ASTROLOGY

Astrologers believe that the positions of the sun, the moon, and the planets at the time of your birth have a big influence on your life. Not only do these positions determine what sort of person you are, they affect the course of your life.

Throughout history some people in positions of power, when faced with tough decisions, have turned to astrologers for advice. Some modern examples: the Shah of Iran, India's prime minister Indira Gandhi, Cambodian president Lon Nol, and American First Lady Nancy Reagan.

There are two main systems of astrology. You can see the first type in a simplified form in the daily horoscope column of your newspaper. It has its roots in ancient Egypt.

The second, the Chinese system, is based on the cycles of the moon and dates back to about 2700 B.C. In our country it shows up mainly on place mats in Chinese restaurants, along with pictures of animals. Both systems are far more complex than newspaper horoscopes or place mats can possibly indicate. It takes lots of time and experience to draw up an accurate birth chart.

THE TAROT

Some fortune-tellers give readings from a deck of ordinary playing cards, but there's a special deck called the tarot, designed especially for telling fortunes. It consists of fifty-six cards divided into four suits—traditionally called swords, wands, cups, and pentacles—plus twenty-two special cards picturing such figures as the Fool, the

A diagram called a zodiac pictures the twelve celestial signs that astrologers say determine a person's personality and fate. The Chinese zodiac associates each sign with a particular animal.

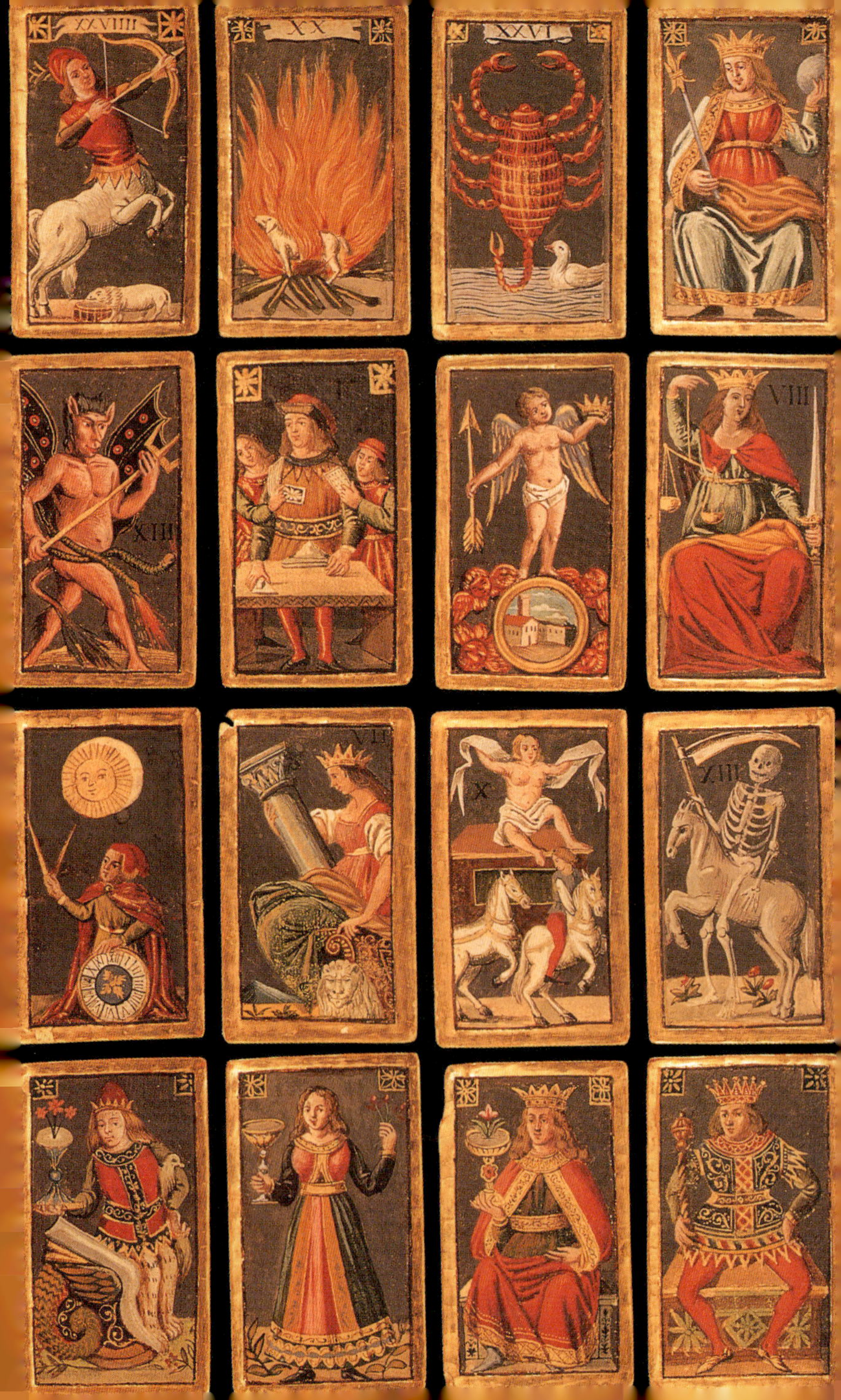
XXVIIII
XX
XXVI

PROPHECY

Hanged Man, and Death. The reader spreads some of the cards out face up in a particular pattern. That's the easy part; the hard part is figuring out what it all means.

SCRYING

The technique called scrying involves looking for images by staring into a mirror—like the evil queen in *Snow White*—or into a body of water, or into the old reliable crystal ball. Actually, any reflective surface will do. Arab soldiers once peered into their polished sword blades for signs of the future.

Though the evil queen used her magic mirror mainly to check up on Snow White, mirrors have a long history as a device for looking into the future.

Opposite: Over the years, tarot decks have been decorated with dozens of designs, some crude and some real works of art. Note that the card bearing the "unlucky" number thirteen represents Death.

For centuries professional prophets and ordinary folk alike have been experimenting with scrying. The idea is to stare into a mirror or pool of water until a foglike curtain appears, along with images that depict future events.

PROPHECY

THE *I CHING*

This Chinese "Book of Changes" may be the oldest book in the world. One legend says it was written by the Emperor Fu Hsi, some 4,500 years ago. Originally, consulting the *I Ching* meant first going through an elaborate ritual of sorting fifty dried yarrow stalks. Now people usually throw three coins a series of six times; the patterns in which the coins fall tell them which page of the book to turn to.

Since about the sixth century, flipping coins has been an accepted method of determining the I Ching's messages. But traditional Chinese seers still use a complex technique that involves sorting and casting yarrow stalks.

FATEFUL FOREBODINGS

The messages in the book are mysterious at best. The one titled "Chung Fu" reads: "Inner truth. Pigs and fishes. Good fortune. It furthers one to cross the great water. Perseverance furthers."

Among the famous people who have relied on the *I Ching* are the psychologist Carl Jung and the Chinese philosopher Confucius, who said that if he had another fifty years to live, he'd spend it studying the *I Ching*. Writer Philip K. Dick plotted an entire novel, *The Man in*

Some palmists claim that, during a reading, they are actually tuning in to the subject's thoughts. Skeptics say palmistry consists mainly of stock phrases, plus some educated guesses based on the subject's manner and appearance.

the High Castle, with the help of the *I Ching*. It worked; the book won a Hugo Award for Best Science Fiction Novel of 1962.

PALM READING

Like the *I Ching*, palmistry started thousands of years ago in China. And, like the other methods of fortune-telling, doing it right isn't a simple matter. Palmistry involves not only the lines on the palm but also the mounds and hollows, the shape of the hand, the fingers and the fingernails, and even the texture of the skin.

Obviously none of these methods is for amateurs. That's why every civilization from ancient Sumer to modern America has turned to professional prophets to scope out the future for them.

Greeks Bearing Gifts

Probably the most famous fortune-tellers were the oracles of ancient Greece. The three greatest were those at Dodona, Claros, and Delphi. At the height of their fame, in the fifth and sixth centuries B.C., people from all over the Mediterranean world came bearing gifts—and questions—for the oracles.

The Greeks of that time believed that our future is decided in advance by our own actions. So it wasn't much of a stretch for them to believe that we can know that future in advance.

The oracle herself, also called the Pythia, was usually an older woman, preferably one who had led an especially pure life. Each oracle had her own method of looking into the future. At Dodona the "client" wrote a question on a lead strip and placed it in a jar. The oracle at Claros drank water from a mysterious hidden spring. According to the ancient Greek historian Herodotus, the Pythia at Delphi chewed laurel leaves, then breathed in gases from a crack in the earth. This sent her into a sort of fit, or trance, in which she babbled so incoherently that it took a group of priests to interpret her answers.

The sometimes mysterious prophecies handed down by the oracle at Delphi prompted Greek philosopher Heraclitus to remark, "The god of Delphi neither revealeth, nor concealeth, but hinteth."

In the early days of the oracles, a visitor had to offer only a cake to get a reply. But as the fame of the oracles grew, their price went up, and an ordinary Greek had to hand over two days' pay. Rich men and royalty brought gold and jewels, hoping to buy a favorable prophecy.

Alexander the Great wasn't so subtle. When he turned up on the oracle's day off and she refused to make a prophecy, he dragged her bodily into the temple and demanded one. To get him off her back, she told him what she knew he wanted to hear: "You are invincible, my son."

Not all predictions were so straightforward. Most of the time the questions people asked were about everyday matters: Shall I marry? Shall I become a sheep farmer? And the answers were a simple yes or no. But the oracles are best remembered for their more cryptic and ambiguous messages.

One of the most famous was delivered by the Delphic oracle to King Croesus of Lydia in 546 B.C. Croesus wanted to know whether it was a good idea to cross the Halys River and invade Persia. The oracle's advice, put into verse by her priests, went something like this:

> *When Croesus has the Halys crossed,*
> *A mighty empire will be lost.*

Naturally Croesus took this to mean that he'd conquer Persia. Unfortunately for him, the empire that was lost turned out to be his own.

As the demand for the oracles' advice grew, handing out prophecies became less of an art and more of a business. Instead of going to all the trouble of a trance, the oracles stooped to quicker, easier methods, such as reading the innards of animals or observing the flights of birds. Their reputation went downhill. People began turning to fortune-tellers who were cheaper and closer at hand.

Emperors and Kings

In early Rome every great family had its personal astrologer. This was a risky line of work; if an astrologer predicted too many unpleasant things, or if disasters happened that he *hadn't* predicted, he might be put to death. Every so often the current emperor got so disgusted with the lack of accurate forecasts that he banned all prophets for a time, and burned their books.

But not all astrologers were inaccurate. Apollonius of Tyana correctly predicted the fates of all seven Roman emperors who ruled between A.D. 68 and 96. The emperor Domitian, upset because Apollonius had foreseen an early and violent death for him, brought the soothsayer to trial. Apollonius foiled the emperor; he'd read his own future, too, he said, and it didn't include being put to death by Domitian. While Domitian pondered this, Apollonius slipped away.

Domitian's personal astrologer, Ascletarion, wasn't so lucky. When Domitian called him in for a second opinion, Ascletarion agreed that the emperor would meet a bad end. Furious, Domitian asked whether Ascletarion could see his own fate. "I shall be eaten by dogs," Ascletarion replied.

Determined to prove the astrologer wrong, Domitian ordered the man's head cut off, his body burned, and the ashes thrown in the river. But just as Ascletarion's funeral pyre was being lit, a sudden storm put out the flames and sent the executioners scurrying for cover. When they returned, they found that a pack of wild dogs had dragged off Ascletarion's body and eaten it, just as he'd predicted.

Julius Caesar was warned of impending danger both by his wife, who had a premonitory dream, and by his astrologer, who somehow deduced the danger by examining the liver of a sacrificial bull.

And what about Domitian's fate? He was stabbed to death by his wife's servants.

The assassination of Julius Caesar was foreseen by several people, including an astrologer named Vestricius Spurinna, who warned Caesar to "beware the Ides of March"—March 15. Caesar was to appear before the Roman Senate on that date.

On the fourteenth, Caesar's wife, Calpurnia, dreamed that she saw her house crumbling and her husband stabbed. She begged him to stay home, but Caesar had always scoffed at omens and prophecies—except those that predicted his success. He ignored the warnings, and was stabbed to death at the Senate by conspirators.

Greece and Rome weren't the only hotbeds of prophecy. In Great Britain the ancient Celts and their druid priests firmly believed in "second sight." The greatest of the Celtic seers was born in Britain around A.D. 415. His name was Merlin. We know him as the mythical wizard from the King Arthur legends. But some scholars believe he was an actual prophet, who foretold events that lay more than a thousand years in the future, such as the reign of Queen Elizabeth I and the French Revolution.

Perhaps the strangest of Britain's prophets was a slow-witted plowboy named Robert Nixon, who lived in the late 1400s. Robert's large head and bulging eyes and bad habit of drooling made him the butt of other boys' insults.

Robert was a lazy lad, so when one day he stopped working and stood staring up at the sky, the overseer assumed he was shirking again, and beat him. Robert didn't even notice. After an hour he came to his senses. Normally he did little more than grunt, but now he spoke eloquently about what he'd seen during his trance. He foretold the English Civil War in the 1600s, the execution of King Charles I, and the French Revolution, along with events of local interest, such as the birth of a child with three thumbs. He even predicted his own future: "I shall be sent for by the King, and starved to death."

Sure enough, King Henry VII heard of Robert's psychic abilities and had him brought to the royal palace. To test him, Henry hid a ring, then told Robert it was lost and asked him to locate it. Robert

The ancient Celtic religion of druidism is still practiced by small scattered groups in the United States and Europe. English druids were allowed to perform their rites at Stonehenge (above) until 1985, when the site was made off-limits because of vandalism.

We know Merlin the magician from the King Arthur stories, but could he have been a real prophet?

FATEFUL FOREBODINGS

replied, "He who hides can find." Impressed, Henry gave the boy the run of the palace. Robert had an enormous appetite and made a nuisance of himself in the kitchen. While the king was away on a hunting trip, the cooks, tired of Robert's demands, locked him up in an unused room and forgot about him. As he had predicted, he starved to death.

Meanwhile, half a world away in Mexico, the Aztecs were using astrology and dreams to peer into the future. One of the devices they used was called *The Book of Good and Bad Days*, supposedly com-

Aztec priests relied on astrology, dreams, omens such as earthquakes and comets, and the prophecies of Quetzalcoatl to foretell the future. Here a priest predicts the future of a child born under the sign of the rabbit.

PROPHECY

piled by the priest-philosopher Quetzalcoatl with the help of the gods. The Aztecs consulted it before beginning any project or journey.

Montezuma, who became emperor of Mexico in 1502, was an accomplished astrologer. For generations Aztec prophets had been saying that one day their country would be invaded by bearded men from across the sea, wearing metal hats and carrying swords. In 1508 Montezuma himself had a similar vision, in which the invaders carried sticks that shot flames and rode what he described as "deer"—no Aztec had ever seen a horse.

In 1519 the vision proved true. The first white men—bearded Spaniards with swords, helmets, and horses—landed in Mexico and destroyed Montezuma's empire.

A hundred years later, in what is now Virginia, another ruler, the Algonquian chief Powhatan, was warned by his priests that his empire would be destroyed by men from the east. Powhatan thought they were referring to the Chesapeake tribe and proceeded to conquer the Chesapeakes. Then, in 1607, he learned the real meaning of the prophecy when three English ships landed, bringing John Smith and his men to settle in the "New World."

Ten Centuries' Worth of Prophecy

At about the time the Spaniards were invading Mexico, a young medical student named Michel de Nôtredame was tending to victims of plague and famine in France. Michel went on to build a solid reputation as a doctor. But what made his name known throughout the world for centuries to come was his skill at telling the future. He's better known as Nostradamus, the Latin version of his name that he adopted when he got his medical degree.

Prophets don't often put their predictions in writing; it's too easy to be proven wrong if the words are down in black and white. But Nostradamus seemed to have no fear of his prophecies being challenged. From 1555 to 1566 he produced ten volumes that he called *Centuries*. Each contained about a hundred four-line prophetic verses. Nostradamus claimed that they forecast events as far off as the year 3797.

The thirty-fifth verse of Book One is probably his clearest and most accurate. Here's a fairly literal translation:

Whatever Nostradamus's powers as a prophet may have been, there's no question that he was an excellent physician—and no slouch as a scientist, either. He supported the revolutionary notion that the earth revolved around the sun.

> *The young lion will surpass the old,*
> *On the field of battle by a strange duel:*
> *In a cage of gold, his eyes will be poked out,*
> *Two kinds one, then to die, a cruel death.*

The prophecy came to pass four years later. King Henry II of France staged a jousting tournament to celebrate the marriage of his daughter. Henry himself challenged a younger man, the count of Montgomery. When the contest was called a draw, Henry insisted on a rematch. This time Montgomery's lance shattered; a splinter flew through the visor of Henry's gilded helmet and into his right eye. A second splinter pierced the king's throat.

Ten days later Henry died an agonizing death. The citizens of Paris accused Nostradamus of sorcery and demanded he be burned at the stake. But Henry's widow, Catherine, found his predictions so valuable that she spared his life.

Very few of Nostradamus's verses are as straightforward as that one. Like those of the Greek oracles, his prophecies are vague and puzzling. Most of his rhymes are so full of puns and symbols, anagrams and obsolete words, that they can be interpreted to mean almost anything—and have been. During World War II both sides enlisted Nostradamus. The Germans pointed to his prophecies as proof that they were destined to triumph. At the same time the British used them as evidence that the German cause was doomed. If Nostradamus's verses didn't quite fit the facts, the astrologers of both armies simply revised them, or made up new ones.

Today Nostradamus's reputation varies according to whom you ask. True believers credit him with predicting everything from the disastrous London fire of 1666 to the end of the world. Some scholars say his verses weren't meant to predict events at all but to make fun of public figures of his own day; he phrased the rhymes in such vague terms to avoid being punished. Skeptics point out that only the most mysterious prophecies can be interpreted to seem accurate.

PROPHECY

When Nostradamus gave specific names and dates, they seldom proved to be true.

James Randi, author of *The Mask of Nostradamus*, composed this satirical verse in Nostradamus's own style:

> *Nostradamus in his four-sided hat*
> *Told his strange tale in a kind of ping-pong.*
> *Hinting at this, making guesses at that,*
> *Too bad for him, but his forecasts were wrong.*

The legends that surround Nostradamus show that he was considered a powerful prophet in his own lifetime, but there were probably plenty of doubters even then. If so, Nostradamus had the last laugh on them. First, he foretold his own death, in 1566. Then, fifty years later, he topped that. As his coffin was being dug up and moved to a more important spot, authorities opened it, hoping he'd buried more predictions with him. He had. On his chest was a brass plate, engraved with that day's date.

Poor Prophets

Since bad news and catastrophes are often the subjects of prophecies, it's not surprising that one of the favorite pastimes of prophets, including Nostradamus, has been predicting the end of the world. Most seers have put the date safely far in the future, when they won't be around to see it. But some have been certain that destruction was just around the corner, and have convinced thousands of followers.

An astrologer named John of Toledo called for the end to come in September 1186. The ruler of the Byzantine Empire took the warning so seriously that he had the windows of his palace in Constantinople walled up.

Beginning in 1499 astrologers throughout Europe predicted a flood of biblical proportions, to come in February 1524. In England, as the date approached, twenty thousand Londoners fled their homes. In other countries people took refuge in boats or climbed high hills. The German Count von Iggleheim helped spread the alarm by building a three-story ark. When the rains failed to show, an angry mob stoned the count to death.

Religious fanatic William Bell proclaimed that the world would

Artists as well as prophets have given us their visions of how the world will end. This 1498 woodcut by Albrecht Dürer depicts the Four Horsemen of the Apocalypse, symbolic figures representing War, Pestilence, Famine, and Death.

Members of a religious sect called Second Adventists listen with grim (or perhaps bored) faces to a speaker predicting the imminent end of the world.

crumble on April 5, 1761. On April 6 his disappointed followers committed him to an insane asylum.

The Southcottian religious sect in England has specialized in end-of-the-world prophecies ever since 1774, when its founder, Joanna Southcott, claimed she would give birth to the "New Messiah," who would radically change the world. When that didn't happen, her disciple, John Turner, scheduled the end for 1820, and his successor, John Wroe, for 1977.

PROPHECY

Not every psychic has been concerned with such earthshaking events. In the late 1700s a man named Bottineau, the lighthouse keeper on the Isle of France, off the coast of Africa, displayed an uncanny ability to predict several days ahead of time when ships would turn up, including how many and from what direction. He called his strange ability "nauscopie." The French government offered him a lifetime pension if he'd reveal how he did it. But Bottineau held out for more money. Eventually the government lost interest, and Bottineau died poor and forgotten.

Predictions as accurate and precise as Bottineau's have always been extremely rare. Throughout history most professional prophets

Prophets of doom are still with us. This one displays his message in London's Hyde Park. The Bible verse he refers to says, "But the end of all things is at hand: be therefore sober, and watch unto prayer."

FATEFUL FOREBODINGS

have had very few "hits" and a whole lot of "misses," and our modern soothsayers are no exception.

Some years ago the tabloid *National Enquirer* kept track of predictions made by well-known psychics over a four-year period. Of 364 predictions, only 4 were correct. That hasn't stopped such modern prophets as Edgar Cayce, Jeane Dixon, and Sybil Leek from attracting large followings. Dixon's fame rests largely on the belief that she predicted President Kennedy's assassination.

There's a long-standing notion that a kind of curse surrounds the American presidency. Every president elected in a year ending with a zero, the story goes, will die in office. For a while the "curse" held true: Harrison, elected in 1840, died in office; so did Lincoln, elected in 1860; and so did Garfield (elected in 1880), McKinley (1900), Harding (1920), and Franklin Roosevelt (1940).

In a 1956 interview Dixon predicted the death of the president who would be elected in 1960—a blue-eyed Democrat, she said, which seemed to indicate Kennedy. But as the election drew near, she changed her mind and predicted that Kennedy *wouldn't* win.

Of course Kennedy did win, and he did die in office. But the president elected in 1980, Ronald Reagan, though he was wounded by a bullet, somehow escaped the "curse."

Even if Dixon really did foresee Kennedy's death, it hardly makes up for her many misses, such as her predictions that Russia would put the first man on the moon, a huge comet would strike the earth in 1980, and China would start World War III in 1988.

How to Be a Prophet

Other cultures have traditionally subjected would-be prophets to a trial by ordeal to see if they were worthy. The Inuit (Eskimos) submerged them in icy water. In some Native American tribes, prophets steamed themselves in a sweat lodge until they nearly passed out from the heat. Nowadays, almost anyone can be a prophet—even you.

In his book *The Mask of Nostradamus*, James Randi gives a list of rules for being a successful prophet. Here's a condensed version:

Rule 1: Make lots of predictions. Gloat over the few that come true, and ignore the ones that don't.

Rule 2: Be vague, not definite; use words like "perhaps" and "I feel that . . ."

Rule 3: Use lots of symbols; they can be interpreted in many ways.

Rule 4: Predict two opposite things, then pick the one that actually happens as your "real" prediction.

Rule 5: Give credit for the hits to God, and blame the misses on human error.

FATEFUL FOREBODINGS

Rule 6: No matter how often you're wrong, keep predicting. Your followers will still believe.

Rule 7: Predict catastrophes; they're popular and easily remembered.

Rule 8: Predict things *after* they happen.

Randi's rules are mostly tongue-in-cheek, of course. But there are some real ways of testing your prophetic abilities. One is to try writing down, at the beginning of the year, a list of a dozen or so things you think will happen that year. At the end of the year, check the list and see how many hits you scored. If you get even one, you're doing better than most prophets!

If you don't really want to be a prophet, but just want to get an occasional glimpse of the future, here are some simple, time-tested methods that anyone can use.

TEA LEAVES

Brew a cup of tea in a white teacup, using loose leaves, not tea bags. Drink the tea, leaving just enough in the cup to cover the leaves. As you swirl the cup three times counterclockwise, think about the problem or question you want answered. Turn the cup upside down on a saucer and let it drain a minute, then turn it right side up, holding it by the handle, and you're ready to read.

If you're patient, and you squint a little, you should be able to make out a few shapes in the leaves. There are lots of possibilities. Here are a few common ones: A full moon means romance; a ball and chain mean unpleasant duties; an arrow means bad news; a mouse

The renowned psychic Eileen Garrett saw no value in reading tea leaves. "To get any picture out of them at all," she said, "requires a most abundantly fertile imagination."

means danger or money problems; a kangaroo means harmony; an airplane means a journey; an angel means good news. The closer the shapes are to the handle, the more the prediction affects you. Shapes near the edge of the cup signify events that will happen soon; those near the bottom are far in the future.

FATEFUL FOREBODINGS

MELTED WAX

You'll need a candle and a bowl of cold water. Light the candle, at the same time asking a question regarding your future, or making a wish. Tilt the candle and let a few drops of melted wax drip into the water. At first the wax will form a border around the edge of the bowl; if the border is unbroken, the outlook is good. A wavy border indicates the future is uncertain. A broken border means there's trouble ahead. Drop in more wax, and it will start to form shapes. Some possibilities: A cat shape means trickery; a pistol means disaster; a ship means a journey or news from far off.

PENDULUM

Suspend a small, fairly heavy object from a string. Hold the end of the string between two fingers and let it dangle. Ask it a question to which you already know the answer is yes. Then watch the movement of the pendulum. Be patient. It may take a few minutes to do anything. Now hold the pendulum still again and ask a question to which the answer is definitely no. Watch how the pendulum reacts. Now that you know what movement indicates a yes and what indicates a no, you're ready to ask the pendulum questions to which you *don't* know the answers.

DICE

Roll three ordinary dice and add up the total of the spots that face upward, then consult this chart to see what the number means.

PROPHECY

3 good luck

4 bad luck

5 a wish will come true

6 loss

7 problems at school

8 problems from outside

9 romance

10 birth

11 parting or illness

12 good news

13 sadness

14 help from a friend

15 be careful

16 travel

17 changing plans

18 great success

You can also try drawing a circle twelve inches across and tossing the dice into it. If one die ends up outside the circle, it means something will mess up your plans; if two stop outside it, it means a quarrel; if all three land outside, it means you shouldn't roll so hard. If you get really ambitious, you can start learning one of the more complex methods of fortune-telling that are covered near the beginning of this book. Nearly any large library or bookstore carries books and materials that can teach you how to read palms or tarot cards, how to consult the *I Ching* or a crystal ball.

Since it takes a lot of time and effort to learn to use these methods right, you'll have to be serious about it. But how seriously can you

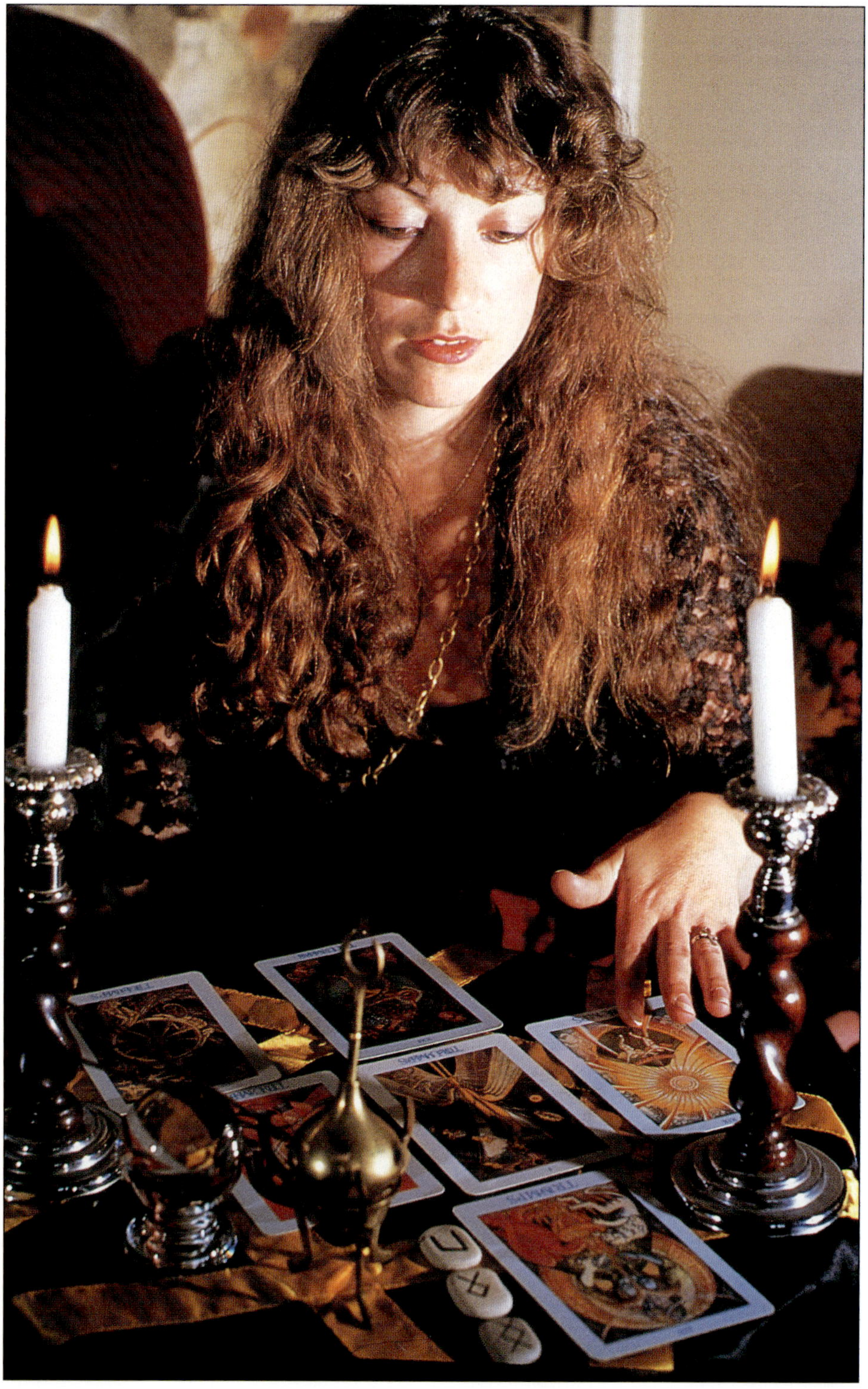

really take the art of fortune-telling? Is it all just a game, or can it really be a valuable tool?

Some scientists say that, by concentrating hard on a question or a problem, you're tuning in to some level of reality that your conscious mind can't grasp. It may be your own unconscious mind, or something called the "collective unconscious." If you read the future of another person, you may somehow be tapping into that person's innermost thoughts and desires—his or her "true self."

Whether or not prophets and fortune-tellers actually see into the future, they can serve a valid purpose: They help people make up their minds. We all have decisions to make in life, often without any good reason for deciding one way or the other. So the advice we get from a tarot deck or a pendulum or a roll of the dice may be as good as any other.

It's uncertain just where and when the practice of reading the tarot began. One eighteenth-century French author believed that the symbols on the cards were devised by wise men of ancient Egypt who compiled them in a book called The Book of Thoth—*a name still sometimes used for the tarot deck.*

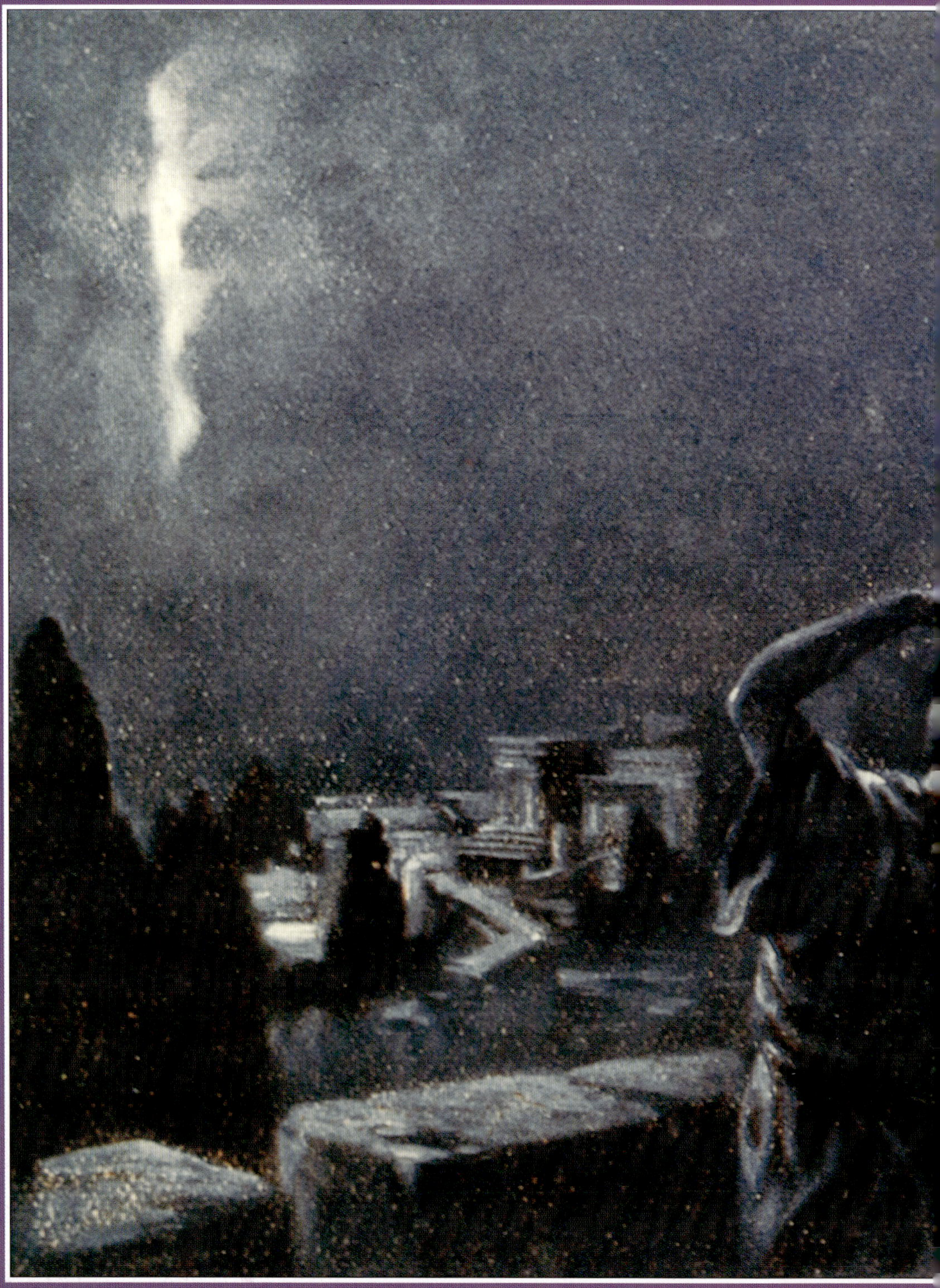

PART TWO

Premonitions

Violent Visions

You don't necessarily have to be trying hard in order to get a glimpse of the future. Sometimes fateful forebodings come to those who aren't looking for them. For twenty-three centuries there have been recorded incidents of people being struck, as if by lightning, by an uneasy feeling, a vivid dream, or a waking vision picturing some event that lies in the near or distant future.

Usually it's something bad. Apparently it's easier to see disaster coming than it is to see good news. But in most cases those who foresee the disaster are powerless to prevent it, either because no one will take their premonitions seriously or because they can't pin down the exact place or time. Time is the hardest part to get right. In the psychic world, time as we know it doesn't exist. Most accurate predictions come true within a few hours, but sometimes it takes days, or even years.

If David Booth's premonition had been more precise, he could have prevented the worst air accident in United States history. In May

FATEFUL FOREBODINGS

1979 he had the same terrifying dream for ten nights in a row. In it he saw an American Airlines jet swerve and roll, then plunge to the ground and burst into flames.

On May 22 he called the Federal Aviation Administration. They did take his vision seriously, but he couldn't give them enough details to determine what flight was in danger, on what day, or at what airport. Four days later, at Chicago's O'Hare Airport, an American Airlines DC-10 rolled over in the air, crashed, and burned, killing 275 people.

Sometimes events carry such a weight of emotion that they impress themselves on more than one person. Some of the worst disasters in history have apparently been seen in advance by dozens of people.

At least twenty-four people got a grisly preview of a disaster that took place in Wales. In October 1966 a mountain of coal-mine waste tumbled down on the town of Aberfan, burying 144 people, most of them schoolchildren. Only a few of those who foresaw the tragedy lived anywhere near Aberfan or knew anything about conditions at the mine. One was a child who drew a picture of the event the day before it happened, complete with a clock showing the exact time of the disaster. The night before it happened, a woman identified as Mrs. C.M. described to seven of her friends a vision in which she saw not only the avalanche of coal, but the rescue efforts, including a close-up look at one of the rescue workers and the schoolboy he saved. When film of the rescue operation was broadcast on television, Mrs. C.M. spotted the same rescue worker and the same terrified boy.

The most famous example of fate foreseen is the story of the

Welsh schoolgirl Eryl Mai Jones dreamed that "I went to school and there was no school there! Something black had come down all over it." The following day an avalanche of coal buried the school, killing Eryl and 127 classmates.

steamship *Titanic*. On April 14, 1912, the giant ship, which its owners called unsinkable, struck an iceberg in the North Atlantic and went down with 1,513 passengers and crew aboard. Among them was a British publisher named William Stead. Ironically, Stead had been warned by two different psychics not to travel on the water that year. To add to the irony, in 1892 Stead had written a short story that described a very similar disaster.

This wasn't the only prophetic story about the *Titanic*. In 1898,

FATEFUL FOREBODINGS

fourteen years before the ship sank, a former sailor named Morgan Robertson published a novel titled *Futility*. He claimed to have written the story while in a kind of trance. It was a fictional account of a huge, "unsinkable" steamship that collides with an iceberg on a cold April night and goes down with most of its passengers. The fictional ship was almost identical to the *Titanic* in size, weight, speed, and number of passengers—even in its name. It was called the *Titan*.

At least nineteen people reported having premonitions about

Other Titanic Tales

Oddly, the *Titanic* disaster was the key to preventing another tragedy twenty-three years later. In 1935 a tramp steamer was headed through the same iceberg-choked waters, on the very date that the *Titanic* had met its end—April 14.

That date also happened to be the birthday of a young seaman named William Reeves, who was standing watch on deck. Though Reeves saw no real sign of danger, the thought of the *Titanic*'s fate spooked him, and he shouted a warning. The captain reversed the propellers, and the steamer churned to a halt—just yards from a huge iceberg that had appeared suddenly out of the dark.

The name of that lucky tramp steamer? The *Titanian*.

Another curious footnote to the *Titanic* disaster occurred years later. In 1975 a family in England was gathered around the television, watching a TV movie based on the famous incident. Just at the suspenseful moment when the ship was about to strike the iceberg, a huge block of ice crashed through their ceiling.

To the astrologer who had warned him not to travel on the Titanic, *W. T. Stead wrote: "I sincerely hope that none of the misfortunes which you seem to think may happen to myself or my wife will happen, but I will keep your letter and will write to you when I come back." He never came back.*

FATEFUL FOREBODINGS

the *Titanic*'s voyage. A few, such as millionaire banker J.P. Morgan, listened to their inner voice and canceled the trip. A sailor named Colin McDonald was so sure the ship would sink that he refused a position on the crew.

The year after the *Titanic* sank, another steamship, the S S *Calvados*, went down in the Sea of Marmara, in Turkey, with everyone aboard— everyone, that is, except the fifty passengers who changed their minds and stayed on shore. Did these lucky few have some kind of advance warning? Possibly so.

In the 1950s a researcher named William Cox studied train accidents and found that most of the time there were fewer passengers than normal on a train that was involved in an accident. For example, when a Chicago train crashed in 1952, there were only nine passengers aboard; the usual number was between fifty and seventy. Cox feels that some of those who would ordinarily have been riding on the ill-fated train got some subconscious message that prompted them to take a different train.

Ignoring the Message

For every person who avoids tragedy by listening, either consciously or unconsciously, to a premonition, there are many more who court disaster by ignoring their forebodings. Some ignore premonitions because they don't believe we can see the future, and some because they don't think we can do anything to change it.

Mark Twain's experience is one of the saddest. As a young man Twain was an apprentice pilot on a Mississippi riverboat, the *Pennsylvania*. Twain was very close to his younger brother Henry and got him a job on the boat as a clerk.

On a trip downriver Twain stayed over in Saint Louis at his sister's house, where he had a disturbing dream. He saw Henry's body lying in a metal casket in the sitting room of the house, supported by two chairs. On the boy's chest lay a large white bouquet, with a single red bloom in the center.

The dream seemed so real that Twain was greatly relieved when he woke and found the sitting room empty. He put the painful dream out of his mind.

FATEFUL FOREBODINGS

The *Pennsylvania* made the rest of the trip safely. But along the way Twain had a violent run-in with the pilot and had to leave the boat when it reached New Orleans. His brother stayed aboard. On the trip north, just outside Memphis, the boat's boilers blew up, killing 150 passengers and crew—including Henry.

Most of the dead were put in unpainted wooden coffins, but the ladies of Memphis, struck by Henry's sweet nature even as he lay dying, took up a collection and bought him a metal casket. One elderly lady placed a large bouquet in the casket—all of white flowers, except for a single red rose in the center.

Twain had the casket shipped to his sister's house. As it was being carried upstairs to the sitting room, Twain had it brought back down, not wanting his sister to open it and see Henry's condition. When he went up to the sitting room, Twain found the two chairs he had seen in his dream, waiting to receive the casket. So he had managed to alter the details of his dream, but not his brother's fate.

Though Twain didn't exactly foresee his own death, he did predict it in a way. In 1909 he told a friend, "I came in with Halley's Comet in 1835. It is coming again next year and I expect to go out with it." The following year, when Halley's comet streaked across the skies, Mark Twain died.

The poet Percy Bysshe Shelley repeatedly had nightmares about drowning. In 1822 he dreamed that a friend, Edward Williams, was calling to him, "Get up, Shelley, the sea is flooding the house." Shelley turned on his friend in the dream and tried to strangle him.

Two weeks later, Shelley and Williams drowned together in the Gulf of Spezia.

PREMONITIONS

In 1947 the great welterweight boxer Sugar Ray Robinson had a prophetic dream about his upcoming match with Jimmy Doyle. He saw Doyle on his back in the ring, staring up at him with sightless eyes, while the crowd cried, "He's dead, he's dead!" Robinson tried to call off the fight. His trainer and promoter protested that he was being foolish, that dreams didn't come true. But it took the assurances of a priest to convince Robinson to go ahead with the fight.

In the eighth round Robinson flattened Doyle, just as he had in the dream. The following afternoon Doyle died from his injuries.

Sugar Ray Robinson's dream of becoming a world-champion boxer came true. So did a dream in which he saw his opponent Jimmy Doyle (right) die as a result of the champion's knockout punch.

FATEFUL FOREBODINGS

Abraham Lincoln was a great believer in omens and fate. Many times throughout his life he told friends he was convinced that he would meet an untimely death at the height of his career.

In 1860, shortly after he was elected president, he saw a double image of himself in a mirror; he took this as an omen that he'd die in his second term as president.

During the second week of April 1865, Lincoln and his wife, Mary, and his old friend Ward Lamon were celebrating the surrender of the Confederate army, and the conversation turned to dreams. Lincoln revealed that ten days earlier he'd had a vivid prophetic dream. Lamon recorded the president's words in his diary.

In the dream, Lincoln said, he heard sounds of crying coming from the East Room of the White House; entering the room, he saw a corpse dressed for a funeral, and a throng of people "weeping pitifully." Lincoln asked one of the guards who the dead man was. "The President," the guard replied. "He was killed by an assassin!"

When Lincoln finished, his wife exclaimed, "That's horrid! I wish you had not told it."

"Well," said Lincoln, "it is only a dream, Mary. Let us say no more about it, and try to forget it."

But Mary Lincoln surely recalled that dream when, a few days later, her husband was shot in the head by John Wilkes Booth as he watched a play at Ford's Theatre.

Listening to the Message

Though Lincoln accepted his fate as inevitable, others have refused to believe that the future is carved in stone and have managed to head off some tragedy by taking action.

Shortly before Lincoln's assassination, Julia Grant, the wife of General Ulysses S. Grant, also had a premonition—not a vision like Lincoln's, just a strong sense of foreboding. When Mrs. Lincoln invited her and General Grant to share the president's box at the theater, Mrs. Grant declined. After the assassination Grant learned that Booth had planned to shoot him as well.

One of the most gripping cases of fate forestalled took place in Ireland, in the early 1900s. On a brief vacation, Judge Matthew Doherty of Dublin stopped overnight in the village of Gorey at an inn called the Jeanne D'Arc. The innkeeper's wife was an unpleasant, grim-faced woman who gave Doherty the shivers. But he was too tired to look for another hotel, so he took a room on the second floor. As he looked out the window, he noticed a ladder set up against the wall

Like Julius Caesar, Abraham Lincoln had advance warning of his assassination in the form of a dream and, like Caesar, he chose to ignore it.

under it. Uneasy, Doherty shoved the dresser against the window.

That night, the judge dreamed that a man climbed the ladder and entered through the window with a knife in his hand. He stabbed the judge to death, then let in the innkeeper's wife. Together they dragged Doherty's body to the stable.

Doherty woke in a panic and, not surprisingly, couldn't sleep the rest of the night. First thing in the morning he paid his bill and fled.

PREMONITIONS

Five years later Judge Doherty got word of a murder just committed at the Jeanne D'Arc. He hurried to the village and found the police questioning the innkeeper's surly wife. The woman insisted the victim had been killed by a companion, who had then disappeared.

Judge Doherty accused the woman and her husband of doing the deed. The husband, he said, had climbed a ladder to the victim's room, stabbed him, and then dragged his body to the stable.

Stunned, the woman asked how he could know all that. Her husband was brought in, and the two confessed to the murder. It was the first time Doherty had seen the innkeeper, but he recognized the man's face at once—he was the knife-wielding man in the dream Doherty had had five years earlier.

If Adolf Hitler hadn't had a premonition, or if he'd ignored it, the world might have been spared the agony of World War II. When Hitler was just a corporal in the Bavarian army, during World War I, he was stationed in a bunker on the front lines. One night, he claimed, he had a dream warning him to get up and get out. He did. Shortly afterward the bunker was reduced to rubble by an artillery shell.

Luckily, the man who helped defeat Hitler was also spared an untimely death thanks to a timely premonition. During World War II, when London was suffering German air raids, England's prime minister, Winston Churchill, was visiting the crew of an antiaircraft gun. As he headed for his car, his aide held open the left-hand door, as usual. But without explanation, Churchill walked around to the other side and got in.

A few minutes later, as they sped through the dark streets, a bomb exploded near the right side of the car, lifting it into the air

FATEFUL FOREBODINGS

and nearly overturning it. Only Churchill's considerable weight kept it upright. When his wife asked him why he'd decided to sit on that side of the car, Churchill replied, "Something said 'Stop!' before I reached the car door . . . I was meant to open the door on the other side and get in and sit there—and that's what I did."

The dream of an Illinois coal miner named Roscoe Harris saved the lives of dozens of his fellow miners. In his dream he saw the elevator cage at the mine break loose and fall, killing the twenty-nine men inside. In the morning Harris ran to the mine just in time to see the cage starting its descent—with only twenty-five miners, not twenty-nine, aboard. Harris shouted for it to stop, and recounted his dream.

The superintendent took the warning seriously enough to hook chains around the cage for safety before sending it down—this time with four more miners. The cage broke loose, as Harris had predicted, but the chains kept it from plummeting to the bottom of the shaft. After the near tragedy, the superintendent confessed the reason why he had believed Harris: The superintendent had had the very same dream the night before.

In another case a dream was responsible for saving the life of a young child. The mother dreamed that a heavy chandelier fell onto the child's bed. Unlike most prophetic dreams, this one featured a clock that showed the exact time—4:35 A.M. When the mother woke her husband and told him, he laughed at her concern. But she was so disturbed that she brought the child into their room anyway. Two hours later, at exactly 4:35, they heard a loud noise and investigated. The chandelier had crashed onto the child's now-empty bed.

PREMONITIONS

Not all premonitions are about matters of life and death, of course. Some are relatively trivial, even funny. The ancient Greek philosopher Socrates was convinced that some presence he called a *daemon*, or guardian spirit, guided him throughout his life and warned him when trouble was coming. Once, as he was walking in the countryside with his pupils, Socrates got one of those warnings and stopped suddenly. His doubting pupils went on along the narrow path, only to find themselves knee-deep in a herd of mud-covered pigs.

Occasionally listening to a dream or vision can pay off very literally. In the 1960s a psychologist named Mrs. Hudson had a series of vivid dreams that involved horse races. In each she heard the name of the winning horse announced. To her astonishment it turned out that both the race tracks and the horses really existed. When she placed bets on the winners from her dreams, she won a substantial amount of money.

Naturally not all premonitions are accurate, any more than all prophecies are. The year after the Aberfan disaster in Wales, a British psychiatrist established the British Premonitions Bureau, hoping to head off disasters like the one at Aberfan by learning about them in advance. In 1968 a similar bureau called the Central Premonitions Registry was set up in New York. Of about eight thousand reports recorded by the registry in its early years, only about forty-eight matched an actual event. And of those accurate premonitions, half were reported by the same six individuals.

Unfortunately, most of the premonitions that come true do so within a few hours, so they're not reported until after the event has happened. In an attempt to speed up the process, the Central Premonitions Registry has set up a web site where Internet users can report premonitions. If you're convinced you've had a genuine prophetic dream or vision, you can contact the registry at http://yaron.clever.net/precog/index.shtml.

    If only a few of those recorded premonitions came true, does that mean the others were just imagination or ordinary dreams? Or were they real glimpses of the future, too, only somehow, between the seeing and the happening, the "future" changed?

Seeing Around the Bend

How is it possible to see into the future, since it hasn't happened yet? Some scientists, including Albert Einstein, have suggested that there is no such thing as past, present, or future—that these are only concepts thought up by humans to make our lives easier.

Others say that when we predict the future, we're really just picking up clues from the present and deducing what's likely to happen as a result—the way a meteorologist predicts the weather.

Physicist Adrian Dobbs believes that events can set off something called a "psitronic wave front," like a sound wave, that spreads out in all directions and can be detected by the brain. That would explain why sometimes people get a clear vision of an event that happened in the past, or of one that's taking place in the present but halfway around the world.

Here's an analogy that may make the concept of seeing into the future (or the past) a little easier to grasp. Imagine you're on a small boat, floating down a winding river—the River Time, if you will. You

Sometimes it's hard to tell whether an accurate prediction is due to precognition or a lucky guess, or is just a trick. In 1977 the magician Rogé sealed a written prediction inside five envelopes, which were opened two days later. The prediction inside matched that day's newspaper headlines.

PREMONITIONS

can see behind you only as far as the last bend in the river, and ahead only as far as the next bend. So you have no way of knowing what's coming up: It could be rapids; it could be a waterfall; it could be pirates waiting to rob you and steal your boat.

Now imagine that you're standing on a high cliff overlooking the river, watching that little boat. From this vantage point, you can see what happens to the boat as it floats along; you can also see what's *going* to happen to it. And if you can yell loudly enough, you can warn the boat's passengers—with any luck, in time to let them put ashore and avoid the waterfall, or hug the far bank out of range of the pirates' guns.

True psychics have a way of putting themselves deliberately on that high cliff and of looking far upriver or downriver. The rest of us just have to muddle along without knowing what's around the river bend—unless we're privileged to have one of those rare flashes of foresight.

But those may not be as rare as we think. Robert Nelson, who established the Central Premonitions Registry, believes that many people have prophetic dreams, but they just don't remember them. A poll of 433 university students in Georgia found that 100 of them had experienced at least one predictive dream; 32 had them often.

Since ancient times people have noticed that animals have a sort of "sixth sense," which tells them when something bad is about to happen. During World War II Europeans kept a close eye on their dogs and cats and even ducks; if the animals acted up, it meant an air raid was coming.

In 1963 zoo animals in Skoplje, Yugoslavia, went wild, roaring

FATEFUL FOREBODINGS

and charging the bars; a few hours later, an earthquake destroyed most of the city.

In cases like these it's possible that the animals weren't using a sixth sense; since an animal's hearing is keener than a human's, it's conceivable that it could pick up the small vibrations that occur before an earthquake hits, or hear an airplane before it can be seen.

But in other incidents involving animals, it seems clear that there's some sense at work beyond the usual five. Shortly before Lincoln was assassinated, his dog raced about the White House, howling miserably. A beagle named Skippy even seemed to foresee her own death. Usually she loved to go hunting with her owner, but one day she had to be dragged along, protesting. As they walked through a field, another hunter mistook Skippy for a rabbit and shot her dead.

If other animals have some inborn ability to look into the future, it's reasonable to think that humans may, too.

If we do, how do we go about developing and using that ability? According to parapsychologist Hans Holzer, the first thing you need to do is learn to relax completely so that your mind is in the right mood to receive messages from that other level of consciousness. That can be as difficult to do as learning to read the tarot. It takes time and practice. Holzer suggests getting away from all distractions, breathing deeply for ten seconds or so, then picturing in your mind a movie screen with the word *relax* projected on it.

Because we're usually most relaxed when we're sleeping, that's the prime time to tune in to the premonitions and predictions channel. So if you want to test your precognitive ability, try keeping

PREMONITIONS

a record of your dreams. Set a notebook and pen beside your bed. As soon as you wake up in the morning, try to recall all the details of what you dreamed, then write them down immediately.

If you can't recall a dream, that doesn't mean you didn't have one. Concentrate on the first thing that crossed your mind when you woke; that may lead you to remember a dream.

How can you be sure if one of your dreams gives you a real look into the future? Obviously the best way to tell is by whether or not it comes true. But if the events in your dream are happening to somebody else, and not you, you won't necessarily know whether they come true or not. Those who have had predictive dreams say they're unmistakable. Usually they come in living color; often they occur night after night; though the dream stirs strong emotions, you, the dreamer, usually don't have an active role in it—you're just an outsider, watching the events unfold.

Changing the Future

Suppose you do manage to get a glimpse of your own future, either through a dream or through one of those methods of fortune-telling you've read about. Does that mean you're stuck with it? Do you have to resign yourself to your fate, as Lincoln did? Or is it possible to change the future? And if it *can* be changed, is it really the future?

It stands to reason that the past can't be changed; it's already happened. But what about the future? If people can see events that haven't happened yet, that seems to imply that the future is already decided for us, that it's a set of predetermined events, just waiting for us to catch up to them.

And yet, as you've seen from some of the case histories in this book, sometimes people do manage to change or avoid what the future seems to hold. So when we get a look at what is to come, maybe what we're seeing is not *the* future, but only a possible future. Maybe we're seeing what will happen *if* we don't take actions to prevent it.

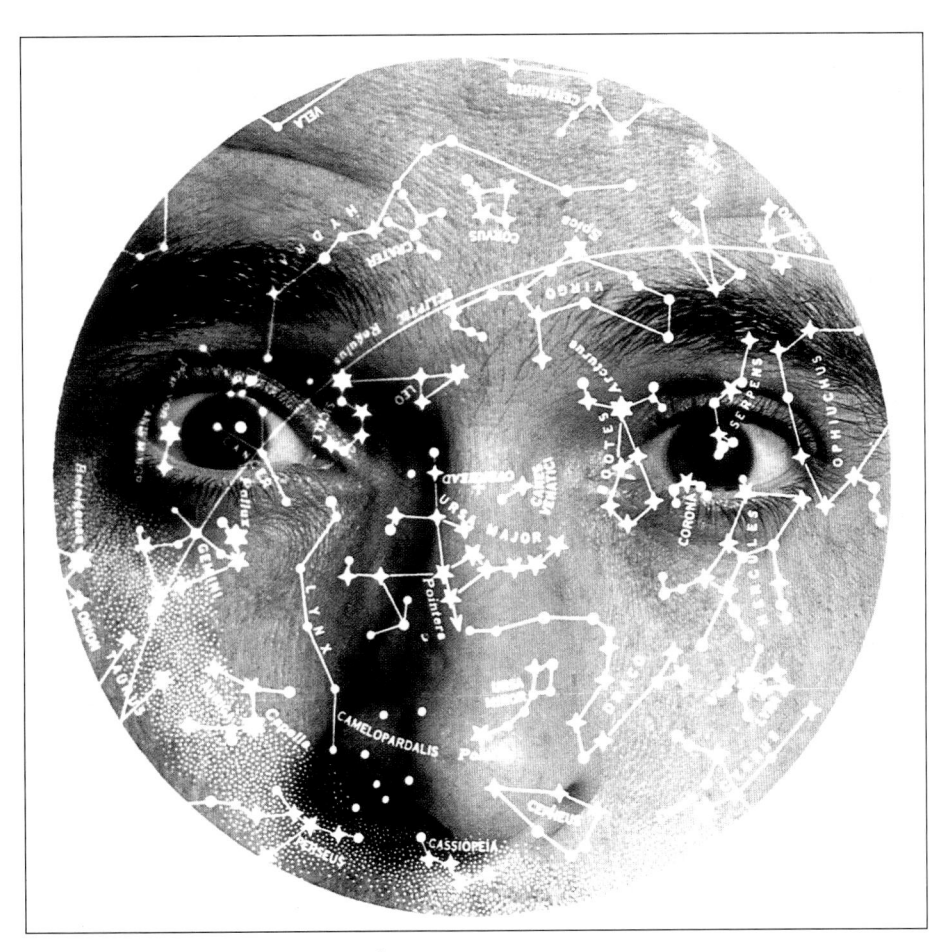

If we do see the future, can we change it?

The Huna religion of Hawaii teaches that the future is decided only up to a certain point; after that, it's just a sort of master plan that can be changed. Followers of the Egyptian god Thoth believed that, when we see into the future, we're getting a glimpse of what challenges we're going to face. If so, that means we can use that knowledge to strengthen ourselves, so we're ready to meet those challenges when they come.

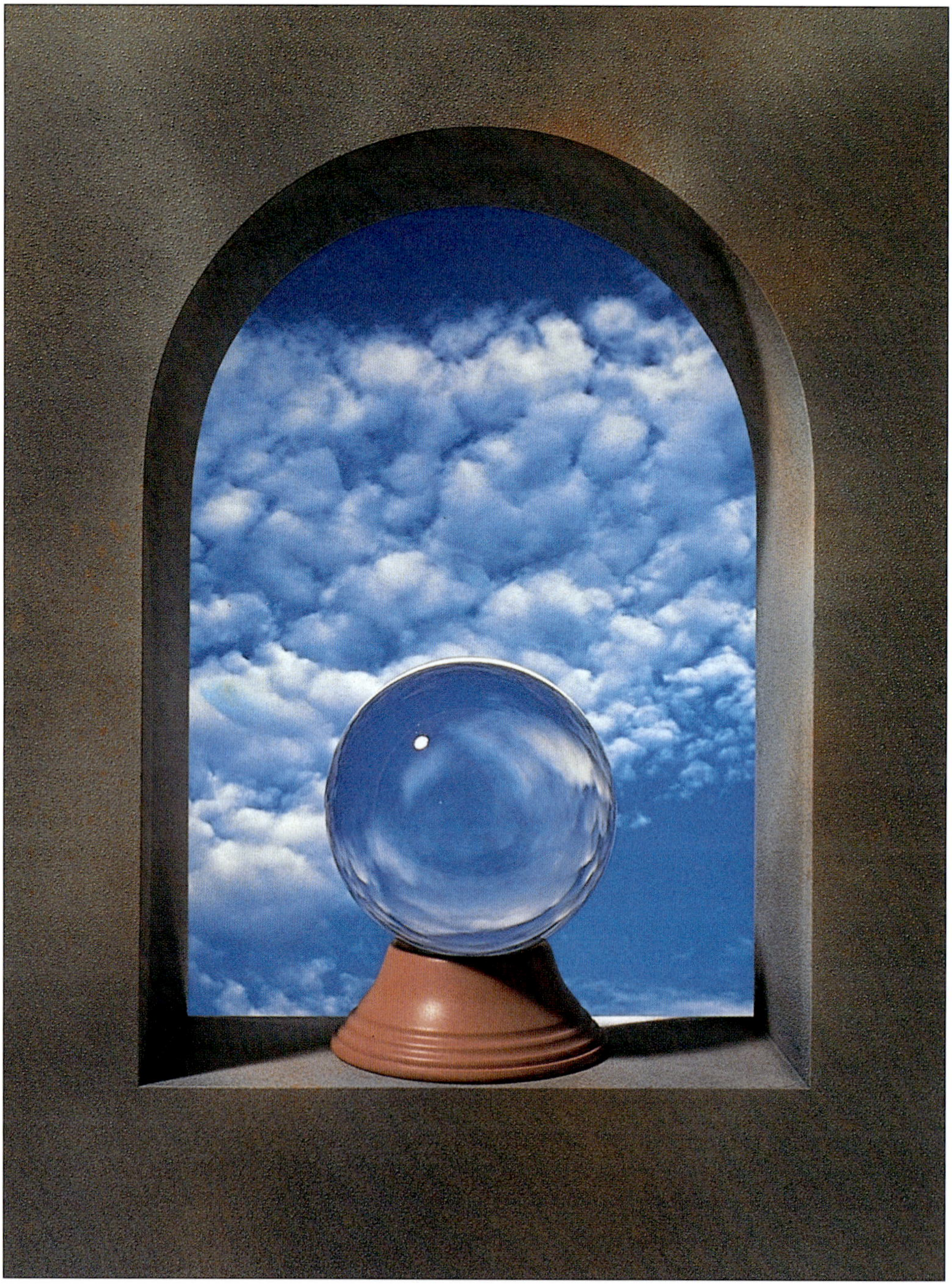

Glossary

Alexander the Great: Alexander III, king of Macedonia from 336–323 B.C. A military genius, he ruled an empire that stretched from Greece to India.

astrologers: People who chart the relative positions of the sun, moon, planets, and stars, believing that they affect our personalities and fates.

Aztecs: A native people of Mexico. During the fifteenth and sixteenth centuries they built an empire that included most of Mexico.

Caesar, Julius: Roman general and historian who became dictator of Rome in 49 B.C. In 44 B.C. he was assassinated by men who feared he would declare himself king.

Churchill, Winston: Prime minister of Great Britain 1940–1945 and 1951–1955.

collective unconscious: A term used by psychologist Carl Jung to describe a fund of knowledge and memories that he believed were inherited by us from our ancestors without our being aware of it.

Confucius (551–479 B.C.): The greatest Chinese philosopher. His sayings were collected in a book called *The Analects*.

Domitian: Emperor of Rome A.D. 81–96.

druids: Priests and scholars of a religion that flourished in Ireland and Britain until about A.D. 500.

FATEFUL FOREBODINGS

Einstein, Albert (1879–1955): German-American physicist best known for his theory of relativity, which states, among other things, that the speed at which time passes can vary.

French Revolution: A bloody, ten-year (1789–1799) revolution that toppled the French monarchy.

Halley's comet: A comet that passes near the earth every seventy-six years, named after its discoverer, English astronomer Edmond Halley.

Henry II: King of France 1547–1559.

Henry VII: King of England 1485–1509.

Hitler, Adolf: Dictator of Germany from 1933 to 1945.

horoscope: Predictions and advice given by an astrologer based on the position of the stars and planets.

Hugo Award: An award given yearly to science fiction authors, illustrators, and publishers. Named for editor and publisher Hugo Gernsback.

Messiah: A savior promised by God to the Jews. Christians consider Jesus that savior and believe that his return will signal the beginning of a new era.

parapsychologist: A person who studies psychic phenomena, such as extrasensory perception and telepathy.

precognition: Accidental knowledge of events that haven't happened yet.

prediction: Making deliberate guesses about the future, usually the future of just one person.

premonition: A feeling of being warned about approaching events; less vivid and specific than precognition.

GLOSSARY

prophecy: Foretelling events, often ones of great importance; sometimes used to refer to divinely inspired visions of the future.

psitronic: relating to extrasensory phenomena.

Shelley, Percy Bysshe (1792–1822): One of the great English Romantic poets; husband of Mary Shelley, the author of *Frankenstein*.

Socrates: A Greek philosopher of the fourth century B.C.; he developed a method of teaching by asking questions.

Sumer: An ancient land in southern Babylonia (modern-day Iraq). The Sumerians, around 3000 B.C., created one of the world's earliest civilizations.

Twain, Mark: The pen name of Samuel L. Clemens (1835–1910), author of *Tom Sawyer* and *Huckleberry Finn*.

yarrow: A wild plant belonging to the daisy family, sometimes used as an herbal medicine.

To Learn More about Telling the Future

BOOKS—NONFICTION

Complete Book of Fortune, The. New York: Crescent, 1990. First published in 1936. An exhaustive encyclopedia of fortune-telling methods for the really serious fortune-teller.

Dickinson, Peter. *Chance, Luck & Destiny.* Boston: Atlantic Monthly, 1976. Only partly about seeing the future, but full of highly entertaining anecdotes, activities, and information.

Edelson, Edward. *The Book of Prophecy.* Garden City, New York: Doubleday, 1974. Succinct but thorough instructions for telling the future by reading palms, dreams, numbers, tea leaves, tarot, *I Ching*, etc.

Gallant, Roy A. *Astrology: Sense or Nonsense?* Garden City, New York: Doubleday, 1974. A substantial and serious look at the history and uses of astrology, written by an astronomer.

Green, Carl R., and William R. Sanford. *Fortune Telling.* Hillside, New Jersey: Enslow, 1993. A quick read; brief descriptions of various fortune-telling methods.

Landau, Elaine. *Fortune-Telling.* Brookfield, Connecticut: Millbrook Press, 1996. A brief introduction to the methods used by professional fortune-tellers.

TO LEARN MORE ABOUT TELLING THE FUTURE

Laycock, George. *Does Your Pet Have a Sixth Sense?* Garden City, New York: Doubleday, 1980. Clairvoyance and homing instincts in animals.

BOOKS-FICTION

Wright, Betty Ren. *The Secret Window*. New York: Holiday House, 1982. Twelve-year-old Meg discovers a talent for seeing things that haven't happened yet.

Zalben, Jane Breskin. *The Fortune Teller in 5B*. New York: Henry Holt, 1991. An eleven-year-old girl finds that her new upstairs neighbor, who has an accent and tells fortunes, isn't as weird as she thinks.

GAMES

Christensen, Amy, and Kirsten Hall. *Madame Boskey's Fortune Telling Kit: A Book and Card Set*. San Francisco: Chronicle, 1996. A set of twenty-four cards, based on Gypsy fortune-telling cards, plus an instruction book. Simple to use, but complex enough to allow for lots of possible readings.

Tremaine, Jon. *Astrology and Predictions Workstation*. Los Angeles: Price Stern Sloan, 1994. Materials and instructions for using various fortune-telling techniques.

Index

Page numbers for illustrations are in bold face.

Aberfan, Wales mining disaster, 50, **51**, 63
Aeschylus, **6**, 7
airline disaster, 50
Alexander the Great, 21-22
animals, 67-68
Apollonius, 23
Ascletarion, 23-24
astrologers, 12, 34
Aztec priests, 28-29, **28**

Bell, William, 34, 36
Book of Good and Bad Days, The, 28, 29
Booth, David, 49-50
Bottineau, 37
British Premonitions Bureau, 63

C. M., Mrs., 50
Caesar, Julius, **24-25**, 25-26
Cayce, Edgar, 38
Celts, 26
Central Premonitions Registry, 63, 64, 67
Churchill, Winston, 61-62
Confucius, 18
Cox, William, 54
Croesus, 22

dice, 42-43, 45
Dick, Philip K., 18-19
Dixon, Jeane, 38

Dobbs, Adrian, 65
Doherty, Matthew, 59-61
Domitian, 23-24, 25
Doyle, Jimmy, 57, **57**
dreams, 67, 68-69
druids, 26, **27**

Einstein, Albert, 65
end-of-the-world prophecies, 34-36, **35**, **36**, **37**

fortune-telling, 11-19, 20, 22

Garrett, Eileen, **41**
Grant, Julia, 59
Greek oracles, 20-22

Halley's Comet, 56
Harris, Roscoe, 62
Henry II, 31-32
Henry VII, 26, 28
Heraclitus, **21**
Herodotus, 20
Hitler, Adolf, 61
Holzer, Hans, 68
Hudson, Mrs., 63
Huna religion, 71

I Ching, 17-18, **17**
Internet, 64

INDEX

John of Toledo, 34
Jones, Eryl Mai, **51**
Junctinus, Franciscus, 7
Jung, Carl, 18

Leek, Sybil, 38
Lincoln, Abraham, 58, 59, **60**, 68

McDonald, Colin, 54
Mask of Nostradamus, The (Randi), 33, 39-40
Merlin, 26, **27**
mining accidents, 50, **51**, 62
Montezuma, 29
Morgan, J. P., 54

National Enquirer, 38
Nelson, Robert, 67
Nixon, Robert, 26, 28
Nostradamus, 30-**31**, 32-33, 34

palm reading, **18**, 19
pendulum, 42
Powhatan, chief, 29
precognition, 5, 7
predictions, 5, 7
premonitions, 5, 7
presidency, American, 38
prophecy, 5, 7
prophets, 34-45
"psitronic wave front", 65
psychics, 38

Quetzalcoatl, 28, 29

Randi, James, 33, 39-40
Reeves, William, 53
Robertson, Morgan, 52
Robinson, Sugar Ray, 57, **57**
Rogé (magician), 66
Rome, early, 23-26

S S Calvados, 54
Scot, Michael, 7
scrying, 15, **15-16**
Second Adventists, **36**
Shelley, Percy Bysshe, 56
Socrates, 63
Southcott, Joanna, 36
Stead, William T., 51, 52-53
Stonehenge, **27**

tarot, the, 12, **14**-15, **44**
tea leaves, 40-41, **41**
Thoth, 71
Titanic disaster, 50-54
train accidents, 54
Turner, John, 36
Twain, Mark, 55-56

Vestricius Spurinna, 25
von Iggleheim, Count, 34

wax, melted, 42
Williams, Edward, 56
World War I and II, 61, 67
Wroe, John, 36

zodiac, **13**

FATEFUL FOREBODINGS

Notes

Quotes used in this book are from the following sources:

Page 21 "The god of": They Foresaw the Future, p. 46.
Page 22 "You are invincible": *Greek Oracles* by Robert Flaceliere (New York; Norton, 1965), p. 10.
Page 22 "When Croesus has": *Natural and Supernatural: A History of the Paranormal from the Earliest Times to 1914* by Brian Inglis (Bridport, Dorset: Prism Press, 1992), p. 55.
Page 24 "I shall be eaten": *They Foresaw the Future: The Story of Fulfilled Prophecy* by Justine Glass (New York: Putnam's, 1969), p. 32.
Page 25 "beware the Ides": *Julius Caesar* by William Shakespeare, act 1, scene 2.
Page 26 "I shall be sent for": *They Foresaw the Future*, p. 100.
Page 28 "He who hides": *They Foresaw the Future*, p. 101.
Page 33 "Nostradamus in his": *The Mask of Nostradamus* by James Randi (New York: Scribner's, 1990), p. 166.
Page 41 "To get any": *Visions and Prophecies* by the Editors of Time-Life books (Alexandria, VA: Time-Life, 1988), p. 45.
Page 51 "I went to": *Charting the Future* by the Editors of *Reader's Digest* (Pleasantville, NY: Reader's Digest, 1992), p. 81.
Page 53 "I sincerely hope": *Cabinet of Curiosities* by Simon Welfare and John Fairley (New York: St. Martin's, 1991), p. 169.
Page 56 "I came in with": *Mark Twain Himself: A Pictorial Biography* by Milton Meltzer (Hannibal, MO: Becky Thatcher's Book Shop, 1960), p. 288.
Page 56 "Get up, Shelley": *They Knew the Unknown* by Martin Ebon (New York: World, 1971), p. 38.
Page 58 All quotes from *With Malice Toward None: The Life of Abraham Lincoln* by Stephen B. Oates (New York: Harper, 1977), p. 426–7.
Page 62 "Something said 'Stop!'": *Mysteries of the Unexplained* by the Editors of *Reader's Digest* (Pleasantville, New York: Reader's Digest, 1982), p. 28.

About the Author

Gary L. Blackwood is a novelist and playwright who specializes in historical topics. His interest in the Unexplained goes back to his childhood, when he heard his father tell a story about meeting a ghost on a lonely country road.

Though he has yet to see a single UFO or ghost, a glimpse of the future or a past life, the author is keeping his eyes and his mind open. Gary lives in Missouri with his wife and two children.